PUFFIN BOOKS

RESULT!

Neil Arksey lives in London, but spends much of his time in a fantasy world. As well as writing books, he works as an actor. He has a soft spot for his two bikes – a skinny racer and a fat-wheeled off-roader. Other passions include rough water swimming, surfing (mostly in his dreams), hill-walking, football, sunsets, chess and curling up with a good book and biscuits.

SURFERS

RESULT!

Neil Arksey

Illustrated by
Ron Tiner

PUFFIN BOOKS

For all my friends and family

PUFFIN BOOKS

Published by the Penguin Group
Penguin Books Ltd, 27 Wrights Lane, London W8 5TZ, England
Penguin Putnam Inc., 375 Hudson Street, New York, New York 10014, USA
Penguin Books Australia Ltd, Ringwood, Victoria, Australia
Penguin Books Canada Ltd, 10 Alcorn Avenue, Toronto, Ontario, Canada M4V 3B2
Penguin Books (NZ) Ltd, Private Bag 102902, NSMC, Auckland, New Zealand

Penguin Books Ltd, Registered Offices: Harmondsworth, Middlesex, England

First published 1999
3 5 7 9 10 8 6 4

Text copyright © Neil Arksey, 1999
Illustrations copyright © Ron Tiner, 1999
All rights reserved

The moral right of the author and illustrator has been asserted

Typeset in Bembo

Printed in England by Clays Ltd, St Ives plc

British Library Cataloguing in Publication Data
A CIP catalogue record for this book is available from the British Library

ISBN 0–141–30206–2

Contents

1 The Other Side 1

2 The Bridge 12

3 Trials and Tribulations 21

4 Hard to Swallow 30

5 School and After 37

6 St Joseph's 47

7 Game 56

8 Argument 69

9 Sunday 81

10 Factory-yard Match 94

11 Honour 106

Chapter One
The Other Side

"LAURENA'S PRETTY."

Ashley kissed his teeth. "Don't be ridiculous!"

"She is."

Ashley laughed.

Thomas spun round to face him. "What's wrong with her then?"

"She's my sister, stupid!"

"Apart from that?"

"You wouldn't understand." Ashley kicked a small stone. It bounced across the grass edge and into the canal. He envied Thomas. Thomas didn't have an older sister. His father wasn't a teacher at Kirkham High.

"You've got to admit, she *is* nice looking." Thomas smirked like an idiot. "She smiles at me."

Ashley groaned. "Don't make me *vom*."

On the other side of the canal there were old warehouses and factory buildings, disused and boarded up. They were fenced off from the towpath, but the fence had holes in it. The dark water of the canal was a graveyard for unwanted bikes, stolen cars and shopping trolleys.

The two boys raced up the steps to the footbridge.

"Look!"

Ashley nodded. More of the fencing had been demolished since their last visit. Another concrete post had been smashed. In the canal, the burnt-out shell of a sports car sprawled piggyback on another drowned wreck.

Thomas threw a stone. "I hate Sundays."

"I love 'em."

"They're so boring."

"Mum goes to church, Dad reads the papers, Laurena gazes at herself in the mirror all day . . ." Ashley flung a stone, high into the air above the canal.

"And you," said Thomas, "you get to hang around down some grotty old canal with me."

"Grotty old you!" laughed Ashley. "Come on!"

Elbowing Thomas in the ribs, he took off at a run towards the end of the bridge.

"Where are you going?"

"Dunno," Ashley kept running. "Just for a poke around and a wander. See what we find."

"I can't." Thomas was following half-heartedly. "I'm not allowed over that side."

"Me neither!" yelled Ashley, taking the steps three at a time. "Let's do it!"

They hadn't passed a soul. The road and broken fence had given way to high factory walls, windowless and drab. Sunlight was gone, you could feel the chill from the dark water; it was deathly quiet, cut off from the world, closed in.

Ashley glanced at Thomas. His feet were

dragging, he kept looking over his shoulder like a nervous bird.

Thomas slowed. "The bridge is nearly out of sight." Broken glass crunched loudly under his trainers. "Shouldn't we turn back soon?"

"You're not *scared*?" said Ashley.

"Don't be stupid!" Thomas made to shoulder-barge him towards the water.

Ashley shoved back. "What then?"

Thomas shrugged. "Nothing."

Ashley walked on. For some reason this forbidden world of abandoned and derelict buildings made his heart beat faster. "It's not far," he called back over his shoulder.

Suddenly, Thomas was interested and scurrying behind him. "What's not?"

Ashley grinned at the ease of his bluff. "Wait and see," he said, quickening his pace.

★

"Listen!"

"What was it?"

Ashley broke into a jog. "Come on!" The shouts and yells seemed to come from all sides. A fight perhaps? There were lots of voices. The high buildings distorted and echoed them, but they were definitely close by. He ran.

"*Curtis!*"

"*Come on you stupid . . .*"

"*Give it to him, man! Give it to him!*"

"*Cas! Cas! CAS!* Over here, mate! Over *here*."

Ashley could hear Thomas pounding the gravel, close on his heels. To his left, the high walls disappeared and the space opened out into a wide factory yard. Grabbing the chicken-wire fence that separated it from the canal, Ashley stared.

"Idiot!"

"Pass it back, man. *Pass* it!"

"Get *rid* of it!"

"PASS!"

How many were there? Fifteen? Twenty-a-side! No – *more*.

"Madness!" panted Thomas beside him.

The boys were large and hard looking, most seemed a few years older. The game was raggedy to say the least pretty much a free-for-all. *On concrete* for heaven's sake!

But what a place! It had to be at least as big as a full-size pitch! There were *thousands* of windows in the old factory buildings surrounding the yard – all smashed. The wire fence had seen better days too.

"Him with the dark curly hair!" Thomas gripped the fence. "Watch him go!"

"Yeah — and he's dangerous in the air too."

Catching the ball on his chest, the boy brought it down without slowing, moved free of the mob and took off, ball at his feet. Effortless.

A pack gave chase. Dodging this way and that, the boy wound his way towards the far goal — a white line painted on the wall. As he drew level with the last defender, he feigned a lurch left, took the ball right and *shot*.

The tall keeper leapt brilliantly to punch the ball clear. The ball ricocheted back off the building.

"Save!" gasped Ashley.

"Corner!" yelled Thomas.

But the ball remained in play. Pushing and shoving, a scrum of boys hacked and kicked. Another shot — the ball leapt back.

And another . . . and another . . .

The ball was finally hooked away.

Thomas turned to Ashley. "Lethal!"

Ashley nodded. "Or *what!*"

After a time, even with so many boys and so few rules, Ashley began to recognize the skilled players. The standard was surprisingly high. The game was being played at an exhausting pace. But it was Cas, the curly-haired boy they had first noticed, who was proving most consistent. In spite of his efforts, the side he captained was losing.

His chief rival, the captain of the other side, was a louder, more aggressive player. He was black, tall as a giant, and built like a tank. His name was Gunner. He had a kick like a missile launcher.

The fence rocked as the ball glanced off the top of an upright and spun towards the canal.

Reacting by instinct – to a blur of shadow in the corner of his eye – Ashley dived.

"*Save!*"

"Nice one!" Gunner ran over. There was blood on his shirt. It was ripped from a fall. "Chuck it."

"Hang on!" panted Cas.

Gunner spun round. "*What's this?* Too bushed?"

Cas put up his hands. "Oh, yeah, *please*. We can't take any more!"

Gunner spat and wiped his forehead.

Cas grinned. "How about some fresh blood?"

Suddenly all eyes were on Ashley and Thomas.

"How about it?" barked Gunner.

Ashley glanced at Thomas. "You bet!" he yelled, tossing the ball sideways.

Thomas got his foot to it. The ball soared up and over the fence. Ashley yanked at a gap in the chicken-wire and clambered through.

"OK." Gunner was already jogging back towards the centre. "The white boy can use his feet – we'll take him. The brother's yours."

Ashley felt a hand on his shoulder.

"How about you?" said Cas. "Can you use your feet?"

He nodded.

"Let's find out," said Cas. "You're kicking with us."

Chapter Two
The Bridge

ASHLEY PUFFED OUT his cheeks.

"You done all right." Cas draped an arm round his shoulder.

"Didn't score any goals."

"Goals aren't everything."

"No." Ashley sighed. "Winning is."

Cas stopped and turned. "Is that what

12

you think?"

Ashley shrugged.

Cas shook his head. "Playing," he said, "not winning. It's playing and *how* you play that counts." He wagged a finger. "Never forget it!"

They slapped hands and shook.

"Players are always welcome," said Cas.

Ashley and Thomas dawdled their way home.

At the bridge they rested on a battered shopping trolley.

"Eleven − nine!" hissed Thomas. He had said little else since the end of the game.

"Yeah, OK! So your side won − big deal! But how many shots on goal did *you* make?"

Thomas dropped his head and grunted.

"My legs," he groaned, "they're *killing* me."

"Me too. Nearly *three* hours!" Ashley hopped off the trolley. "And they were already well into the game when we arrived. What must they be made of?"

Thomas stretched out a leg. "Don't know about you," he gasped, rubbing, "but my last day's going to be spent doing absolutely nish!"

"Squat–diddley!"

"Nothing!"

"Zero!" Ashley flung a stone across the water. "*Freedom!*"

"Not for much longer," said Thomas.

The stone clanged against the bridge. A new school year meant football trials. Ashley's father, Mr Grant, was in charge of Year 8 soccer. Wednesday was crunch day. The trials.

"You're lucky."

"Lucky?" Ashley jerked round. "I don't think so!"

"Your dad'll put you in goal."

"Exactly! I can't understand why anyone in their right mind should *want* to be a goalie."

Thomas crouched, goalie stance. "You get plenty of time on your own . . . on a good day."

"Great!" Ashley sneered. "To daydream you're somebody else, somewhere more exciting."

"Goalkeeping is a specialist job."

"What – and playing midfield, defence or up-front isn't?"

"OK, but at least goalies don't have to run around, non-stop, the entire match."

"That's true." Ashley pretended to dribble an imaginary ball. "Is that the best you can come up with?"

Thomas scratched his head. "Only the goalie gets to wear psychedelic shirts with padded elbows."

Ashley chuckled. "And gloves!"

"Yeah, see! What's so *bad* about goalkeeping?"

"The standing around, for starters," said Ashley, "it can get *very* cold."

Thomas nodded.

"Sometimes a goalie has to stop himself from getting bored," said Ashley. When all of it's happening down the other end, he needs to keep his mind on the game. You have to be able to keep your eye on the ball. You have to be able to coax yourself. You often have to quickly switch from relaxed to ready for action. And you need to be thick-skinned — a hostile opposition crowd behind you, *hating* you, willing you to mess up, has got to be one of the scariest things."

"It's a tough job!"

"Yeah, but somebody's got to do it." Tapping his imaginary ball, Ashley flipped it up. "A goalie is the focus of much hatred and little love. I read that. You're blamed for letting in goals, often blamed for losing the match, but when do you get credit for saves? It's a tough job all right. It's tough, it's *thankless* and *I* don't want to do it!"

He made as if to strike the imaginary ball. Thomas feigned a save. Dodging past, Ashley took off, running towards the fence. "Come on!"

"Where you going?"

"The broken fence post," he yelled, "let's drop a piece of concrete!"

A fat lump of rock with a twisted

rusty core – it was heavy. The two boys shuffled, grunting and puffing.

"One . . ."

"Two . . ."

"Three . . ."

"Raah!"

Ka-PLOSH!

"That was . . ."

"Yeeeeah!"

The ripples spread. By the bridge, they were almost too small to see.

"He thinks I'm fat and useless," said Ashley.

"What?"

"Dad. He's always pushed me into playing goal – says I haven't got the 'physique' to play anywhere else. Thanks to him having a word with Mister Saddler, goal is where I ended up all last year. And now . . ."

"Fat?" Thomas lifted up his jersey. "Show me! I've got more than you."

Glancing at Thomas, Ashley eased up his shirt.

"See!" jeered Thomas, extending his belly. "You've got nothing! I should be the one in goal!"

"Dad doesn't see things that way."

"That's because you're good."

"Because he made me." Ashley slapped his stomach. "It isn't where I want to be."

"I'd love to be in your boots."

"You reckon?" Ashley shook his head. "You wouldn't, believe me. Anyway, there's nothing to stop you. You've got the skills."

"You think so?"

"I *know* so. You just need to prove it – get noticed."

Thomas dropped his gaze. "Would you put in a word for me?"

"I'll have a go. But, to be honest, Dad only sees and hears what he wants. You've got to put yourself forward. You'd do better talking to him yourself."

Chapter Three
Trials and Tribulations

"COME ON, AT the back there – pick up those feet! Get a move on. *Shift!*"

Ashley willed his legs to go faster. They ached. Ahead, a ribbon of boys pounded past the corner flag. Lanky Rawlinson was way out in front, stretching his lead with an easy stride. Ashley himself was somewhere in the back third. A handful of stragglers panted and wheezed behind him. He could feel Dad's eyes.

"The last three", bellowed Dad, from the centre of the pitch, "get to run the whole thing again. How's that for an incentive!"

Boys murmured and groaned. The pace quickened.

Ashley glanced round. Thomas, normally faster than him on long distances, was near the back, his face screwed up with pain. Only Ganesh, Barnett and Lees were behind him. Sunday's mammoth game appeared to have really done Thomas in.

"Come on, you saps! Come on, you crisp-eating, coke-swilling, couch potatoes. *Move it!*"

One final length of the pitch to go.

Now was the moment to squeeze out a finishing spurt. Arms pumping, lungs gasping, Ashley drove his legs faster. And faster . . .

"Aaagh!"

"Ashley Grant! Don't give up, boy. You can't stop there."

"Aaagh!" The pain in his stomach was searing — too tight to straighten up. Ashley remained bent over as muddy boots thundered past.

"You haven't *finished*!" Dad's voice was furious. He was close. "It's to the goalpost."

"I can't."

"No such word."

Ashley slowly straightened. "Sorry," he grunted. "It's a really bad stitch."

Dad's face darkened in a scowl. "Stitch!" he hissed, murderously. "I'll give you stitch!"

Pain stabbed like a knife in the gut. Ashley hobbled, winced and gritted his teeth. He tried again.

"Pathetic! Whine and whinge all you like." Dad shoved him from behind. "You'll finish like all the others. I'll not have you embarrass me in this manner! When you reach the goalpost, you can set off round the pitch again."

I hate him. I hate him. I hate him.

All the way round, Ashley kept himself going by trying to imagine *really* embarrassing things happening to his father. His shorts elastic snapping, for example. Him tripping and falling face first in the mud, bum exposed. You could understand someone being embarrassed about *that*. If that happened, a little rage would be forgivable.

Only when Ashley reached the posts at

the furthest end of the pitch did the painful stitch start to ease off. It had been torture. Dad had not, as threatened, made three boys run again. Just him. Just to double the humiliation.

The rest of the boys had been divided into groups. Now, under Dad's watchful gaze, they dribbled back and forth and ran through skills routines. As Ashley staggered his way down the final stretch, he caught Thomas's eye. Thomas gave a discreet and sympathetic shrug.

"Right – that's enough! Gather round, lads. Chop-chop! Gather round!"

Ashley slumped on the wet grass with the others. Surprise, surprise. It didn't look as if he was going to be given a chance to prove his skills.

"OK. Rawlinson."

"Sir?"

"Right wing."

"Sir."

"Adams."

"Sir?"

"Take the left."

"Yes, sir."

"Barnett."

"Where do you normally play, Barnett?"

"Right back, sir."

"That's you then."

"Thank you, sir."

"Don't thank me. Just prove yourself worthy, Barnett, that's all I ask."

"Yes, sir."

The names and positions rolled on.

"OK. That just leaves the reserves to pick –" Dad peered at his clipboard – "and goalie. Anybody unhappy so far with what they've got? Anyone feel they've been unfairly left out?"

Ashley glanced around.

Thomas was keeping his eyes down.

"Sir . . ."

"What can I do for you, Grant?"

Ashley swallowed and met his father's gaze. "I'd like a chance to trial as a forward . . . sir."

"A forward, eh?" His father's eyes flitted over the watchful faces. "Forwards need to be able to run."

There were a few titters.

A dark smile curled his father's lips. "You had your chance, Grant."

"I got a stitch, sir."

"He got a stitch!"

This time the titters were louder.

"Grant, a boy of your fitness should think himself lucky to even be considered for the team. Don't you think?"

Laughter.

Ashley dropped his head, face and ears burning.

"Anyone else? No? Right, let's deal with the goalie and reserves."

Ashley caught Thomas's eye.

"Sir . . ." Thomas's voice wavered.

"Who's that?"

"Me, sir." Thomas waved half-heartedly.

"Ah, yes. Moffat, isn't it?"

"Yes, sir." Thomas grinned.

"Don't smirk like an idiot, Moffat. What is it?"

"I . . ." Thomas lowered his head. "I'd like to try for goal, sir."

"What was that? It's no good whispering to the grass."

"Sorry, Mister Grant – sir. I said I'd like to try for goal, sir."

"Goal, Moffat? Would you, indeed?"

"Yes, sir. If that's OK."

28

"If that's OK! Credentials?"

"What, sir?"

"Credentials, Moffat. What experience do you have in that position?"

"You mean like in teams, sir?"

"Yes, Moffat – like in teams."

"None, really, sir. I was reserve last year, sir, with Mr Crabshaw."

"Were you, indeed. Well, I see no reason to question Mr Crabshaw's judgement. You'll stay where he put you." He glanced at his clipboard. "Left-back. Grant will be team goalie. But should anything happen to him, Moffat, you are our reserve keeper. Anyone else got any questions?"

Ashley stared at his boots and chewed his lip.

"Good. I take it that means everyone's happy."

Chapter Four
Hard to Swallow

"EAT UP YOUR toast, Ashley, honey." Mum poured a mug of tea and placed it beside his plate.

"I'm not hungry."

"That's not like you, pumpkin. Breakfast is important. We must all eat to keep our strength up through the day."

30

Dad's newspaper twitched.

Ashley shifted uncomfortably.

"Is something wrong, darling?" Placing both her hands on his shoulders, Mum began rubbing and squeezing. It felt soothing. She worked her way up to his neck. "If something's troubling you, you must tell your mamma."

Dad lowered his paper and glared.

"Mum!" Shrugging away her hands, Ashley reached for the toast.

Dad made a loud throat-clearing, coughing noise.

Mum lifted her eyebrows. "Yes, mih dear?" She retreated into Jamaican at the slightest hint of tension.

Dad frowned. "Just . . ." He breathed out grumpily, through his nose. "Just let the boy get on, or they'll be late for school."

"Yeah." Laurena smirked. "Get a move on, Ash."

Ashley stared at his toast. In spite of the butter and honey, it tasted dry. He was chewing, but he couldn't swallow. Scowling at Laurena, he took a swig of tea. And gulped.

"I'm not happy . . ."

"Ashley?" Mum put down her tea. "Not happy?"

Laurena stifled a snigger.

Dad folded his paper. "Sorry, did I miss something? What did he say?"

"He said he's not happy." Laurena grinned.

Ashley twisted his fingers.

"Not happy?" Dad leant forward.

"I'm . . . I don't think . . ." Ashley was afraid to meet Dad's gaze. "I don't think the trials were fair."

Dad's frown deepened. "Is that right?"

Ashley nodded.

"Well, I'm keen to hear your reason." The familiar sneer curled his lip. "Especially given *my own son* is one of those I've picked."

"The thing is . . ." Ashley cleared his throat. "I'm as good a player up-front as half those you picked. But *I* didn't get a chance to prove it."

Across the table, Mum fixed Dad with an inquisitive glance. Dad shrugged. "As I recall, everyone was given the same chance. Ashley fell at the first hurdle."

"I had a stitch."

"Ashley . . ." Dad shook his head. "Ashley, the modern game is, above all things, about *stamina* and *pace*. At the end of the run, you came in last. If I'd chosen you as a forward over one of your team-mates," he chuckled scornfully, "I might rightly have been accused of poor judgement and favouritism."

"But —"

"No buts." Dad cut him off. "Your goalkeeping skills are proven. But don't forget — your friend Moffat is more than keen to jump into your boots. You should be grateful I didn't choose *him*."

Grateful! He snatched a glance at Mum.

Mum shrugged. "Mih sure what 'im say is for the best."

"Ashley's a wannabe striker, Mum. A wolf in sheep's clothing, aren't you, Ash?" Laurena nudged his foot under the table. "Underneath that soft exterior lurks a *beast*!"

Dad and Laurena grinned at each other across the table, sharing the joke.

"He's a goalie. The team's goalie. That's

good." Mum patted Ashley's hand. "Goalie's what you're good at, isn't it?"

"It's not *all* I'm good at!" Blood thumped in his ears. "It's not what I want to be!" He had to let the pressure out, his head was going to burst. "Dad's never given me a chance." He looked Dad in the eye. "You always say goalie's all I'm good for, but I'll show you!" He kicked hard, under the table.

Laurena screamed.

Ashley snatched up his school bag and stormed from the table.

"He kicked me, Dad, he deliberately *kicked* me."

"Ashley!"

"I can feel it – it's going to be a whopping great bruise."

"*Ashley!* Get back in here this minute and apologize!"

Slamming the front door, Ashley hurried down the path.

Chapter Five
School and After

"GRANT!"

"Yes, miss?"

"Grant, are you off with the fairies?"

"Sorry, miss? No, miss."

"You could at least try to look as if you're paying attention."

It'd been the same all day: staring into

space, zero concentration. In his head, endless re-runs of the football trials and the clash at breakfast. Over and over. Ashley couldn't seem to shake it off.

Dad had been so unfair. But, of course, he was *always* right. When had it ever been different? As for Laurena, Ashley smiled to himself. The kick under the table had been long overdue. Dad adored her and she sucked up to him. It was pathetic. *She* could get away with murder. In arguments or disputes, she and Dad always sided together against him. They were forever mocking him, teasing him and putting him down.

Mum was kind of his ally, but she didn't like arguments and believed in "turning the other cheek". His battles were his own. He had to prove himself alone.

He'd spied Dad and Laurena driving into the staff car park just a few minutes before school. Dad had looked stormy. Avoiding them both at break times had been easy enough, but he'd been growing more and more tense as the day went by. To walk off like that, with Dad ordering him back! If Dad came and called him out of class for a talking to, he would die of embarrassment. Sooner or later, he was going to have to face him.

He stared at his watch and counted seconds to the bell.

Drrrrrrrrrrrrrrrng!

"You can't say I didn't try . . ."

Ashley patted Thomas on the back. "You did all right."

"He's fierce!"

"Tell me about it!" said Ashley.

"Anyone'd think he'd fallen out of bed – on the wrong side!"

"That's everyday Dad. That's what I have to put up with."

As they reached the school gates, Ashley spotted his sister up the road with a group of her girlfriends.

Thomas threw him a sympathetic look. "Good luck," he said, sheepishly.

Ashley tried to smile. "Thanks. I'll need it."

Laurena hadn't noticed him. She and her friends were far too busy. Gathered in a huddle, they chattered, fiddled with their hair and adjusted their clothing. Their jabbering and jostling was punctuated by fits of loud giggles.

As Ashley drew near, the source of their excitement became apparent. Across the road a group of older boys were tapping a football back and forth.

"Oh, here's your little brother!"

Laurena's eyes flashed. "My *big bother*, don't you mean!"

The girls laughed.

Ashley scowled.

"We're just chatting," said Laurena. "*Girls'* talk." Her friends giggled and nudged each other. "You'll have to hang around a minute."

He shrugged. "OK."

The girls turned their backs. He propped himself against the fence and watched.

Across the road, the ball was being kept in the air. The older boys were trying to be skilful, hoping the girls would be impressed. Laurena and her friends weren't interested in the football.

"The one with the wide shoulders is nice!"

"No! The one with the curly hair — he's gorgeous! Look!" Laurena sighed.

Ashley stared. The boy balanced the ball lightly on the end of his foot, flicked it up and headed it. It was Cas!

"Yo!" Cas waved. "All right, mate."

The ball soared over the girls' heads. Dropping his bag, Ashley stepped away from the fence, sidestepped and caught it on his chest. He bounced the ball from one knee to the other. The girls turned to watch. Getting his foot under, he whacked it full power. It rocketed upwards, slowed and began its descent.

Cas and his mates whistled and cheered. The ball dropped like a stone, landing, from its great height, right between them.

"Yeah!"

"Nice!"

Laurena and her friends giggled and huddled once again.

Ashley froze. A familiar red Fiat was

nosing its way out through the school gates. Dad glared through the windscreen. The horn sounded, impatiently. "See you, Cas." Waving across the road, Ashley broke into a trot.

The wave was returned. "Yeah. Laters, mate. Laters!"

For once, Ashley didn't mind the fact that Laurena had nabbed the front seat. Being out of sight, tucked away behind Dad, there was a chance he might avoid his attention.

Dad was glowering through his window. Across the street Cas and his friends were now chatting to the girls.

"Dad!" Laurena shrank into her seat. "You're not going to *say* anything, are you?"

"Those boys aren't from Kirkham," said Dad.

"It's a free country," said Laurena.

Dad grunted. "We can't have their type hanging around the school gates. You can see they're up to no good – shouting from street corners, laughing and kicking a football about. I'm sorry, but I have a duty."

Dad pulled into the kerb between Laurena's friends and the group of boys.

In the back, Ashley tried to make himself invisible.

Dad's window whined and whirred, sliding its way down into the door. Cas and his friends stared irritably at the car that was interrupting their conversation.

"Excuse me." Dad's voice sounded particularly loud and pompous. "These girls have homes to go to and homework to do. You probably have homes to go to too."

The boys looked at one another and smirked.

"Are you offering us a lift?" said Cas.

"No!" snapped Dad. "I am *not*. Boys your age should know better than to play football in the street."

"We were just having a bit of fun," said Cas. He picked up the ball and smiled. "You're right, mister, we were setting a bad example to younger kids – none of us stopped to think. There's better places to play."

Cas's smile, Ashley realized, was now directed at him. He grinned back.

"We have a game every Sunday, kick-off's at two, anyone can join us."

Dad nodded.

"The trouble is, sometimes, between games, we get the itch to kick." Cas eyed the ball. "Know what I mean? I'm really sorry, I'll make sure it doesn't happen again."

Dad stared, at a loss, apparently, for something to say.

The boys stared back.

"Very good," said Dad, finally. He revved the engine.

The car lurched up the street. Ashley was thrown against the seat. Laurena glanced back at him and winked.

Chapter Six
St Joseph's

"RUN WITH IT!" Ashley's breath condensed in great clouds. He balled a fist, clasping it and smacking it with his other hand. That had been his first real slip-up. Why had he *punched* the ball? Why, when he could have made a snatch?

The midfield had been letting ball after

ball through. The pressure had been mounting this half and he was tiring. He had to concentrate. Next time it could be fatal.

His team-mates, in their black and yellow, were charging into the opposition half.

"Come on now, Kirkham! Give it all you've got! Give it ALL YOU'VE GOT!" Dad raced along the touchline, waving his arms and bellowing, like a man chased by bees. "What the *blazes* are you waiting for, Hughes?"

From a great ball by Trease, Hughes the human dynamo now thundered up the middle, well into the other half and still rolling. Purple-shirted opposition converged from all sides.

"Man on, Hughes!" Dad hopped and flapped. "Pass it, boy. PASS the blasted thing."

Too late! Another opportunity wasted. Ashley blew on his gloved hands. The moment of lost possession was a dangerous time.

Now purple shirts appeared on both wings. Purple shirts burst through the middle. Outflanked and wrong-footed, Kirkham were caught on the run. Trease, his long legs striding, shouted orders to retreat.

"Get back, you idiots. Tackle him, somebody!" From the touchline his father yelled, hands cupped to mouth. "Come on, Trease! Moffat, do your job!"

Ashley crouched and waited.

"Come on, St Joseph's!" The opposition coach jumped and roared. "Come *on!*"

Their tall centre-forward had the ball. He had taken more than his fair share of shots this game, three of them on target and tricky to save. Thomas matched him for height, but not speed. Ian Barnett, the right back, matched neither. The earlier efforts of the two defenders had not been promising. Barnett was hanging back and looking the wrong way.

"Go out to meet him, Barny!" Ashley shooed, frantically. "Go on – tackle!"

The attacker had options on both flanks, and four team-mates immediately behind. Ashley glanced at the boy's face. Which way was he going?

He planned to take it all the way.

Barny's sliding tackle was desperately half-hearted. The centre-forward ploughed on, barging Thomas aside.

Ashley glued his eyes to the ball. This was one-on-one. Just a few short minutes away from a clean sweep.

"It's all down to you, Grant!"

Take the initiative.

The centre-forward swerved.

Too late! Make him go left!

Side-stepping right, Ashley slapped his gloves and growled.

Bosh! Jet-propelled, the ball curved in towards the left.

He dived.

"Saved!" Barny ran over with both thumbs up.

"Sorry." Thomas shrugged. "He was going flat out."

"Don't worry about it!" Ashley waved him away. "It's their corner. Come on, mark up! *Come on!*"

Purple shirts flooded the penalty area.

"*Come on, Kirkham!*" Dad ran up towards the corner flag. "Everyone back! Just a couple of minutes left. We're holding on to this one."

Players pushed and jostled for space.

"Hughes." Ashley beckoned the centre-back. "Take the far post."

St Joseph's left-winger paced back for the run up.

"Don't let me down!" yelled Dad. "Ashley – I'm counting on you!"

I know you are.

The ball floated up, curving out over the players at the edge of the box. He sprinted . . .

. . . leapt . . .

. . . and clasped it with both hands. Grunting players crashed into him from all sides. He fell, folding himself around the ball. Colliding bodies tumbled on top.

Blasts on the whistle had never sounded so beautiful.

'Played, Ash. You saved our bacon." Thomas put out his hand.

Ashley slapped it. "Thanks." He smiled. "Just doing my job."

"You deserve a medal." Hughes patted him on the back. "Acting over and above the cause of duty!"

"Yeah, you did all right," said Trease. It's a shame the same can't be said for the rest."

Ashley shrugged. "Let's see what 'sir' has to say."

Sprawled chattering on benches, Kirkham Year 8s dragged off sodden shirts and mud-caked boots.

"One–nil." Dad took up his favourite stance – middle of the room, arms folded. The team fell silent. Turning slowly, he eyed them one by one. "What do we have to say about that?" He fixed on Trease.

"We didn't deserve the win, sir." Trease lowered his eyes. "We could have done a lot better. If it hadn't been for Ashley —"

"Ah, yes!" Dad cut him off. "Ashley." Dad turned. "Bit of a disaster, punching it away earlier."

What? What about the saves?

Dad glowered. "Too slow off the mark. You very nearly lost us our lead. I expect *better*. Still . . . He held out his arms and turned in a gesture of embrace to the rest of the team. A rare smile brightened his face. "We're through to the next round of the inter-schools cup, lads. And, at the end of the day, that's what counts! Trease, well played! Rawlinson, 'Man of the Match' for that goal. Now, get in those showers and scrub! I'll see you back on the coach."

Ashley made a thumbs-up to Rawlinson. The goal had been much needed. A lucky break though, rather than something special. Or was that sour grapes?

Beneath his blond fringe, Rawlinson grinned back. "You did all right, Ash. Your old man's out of order."

Chapter Seven
Game

"WHAT DO YOU mean, you can't?"

"I'm not allowed to cross the bridge. You know that."

Ashley dug his trainer into the bristles of the doormat. "That didn't stop us last time."

"That game was probably just a one-off anyway."

"It wasn't. They play every Sunday." Ashley glanced at his watch. "Kick-off's at two – Cas told me. Come *on*. If we get there early enough, you might get a chance to play in goal. Or are you worried your team might lose if you do?"

"No!" Thomas scowled.

"What then?"

Thomas nodded towards the street.

Ashley turned. Rawlinson, Trease, Hughes and Barnett were crossing.

"A few of us are going to the park," Said Thomas. "With Kirkham getting drawn in the same group as Mawdsley, Treasy thought we ought to start putting in some extra practice."

Trease walked up the path. "Ashley." He nodded. "Good thinking, Thomas. We could use a goalie."

"Not this one," said Ashley. "No offence, but I'm not interested."

"Nobody's forcing you." Trease shrugged. "But if you want the practice, you know where you'll find us."

"Thanks." Ashley pushed past. "I goalkeep because I *have* to. I don't *choose* to." Pausing at the gate, he glanced at Thomas. "Moffat would make a great keeper, given half a chance."

Ashley couldn't resist flinging a couple of stones from the bridge. Checking his watch – one fifty-five – he set off down the steps at a trot. The air had a soft warmth that felt almost miraculous after a week of icy autumnal downpours. A crisp blue sky reflected off the water, making the canal appear less gloomy. A few minutes along the way, he spotted a lone figure kicking a ball. The walk was familiar. Ashley broke into a run.

Cas turned as he approached. "In a hurry?"

Gasping for breath, Ashley staggered to a halt. He nodded.

"Keen, eh?" Cas grinned. "You never told me your name."

"Ashley Grant. Ash."

"I suppose you know mine?"

Ashley nodded.

"So, where's your mate, Ash?"

"Thomas?" he panted. "I called for him, but he wasn't up for it. His parents don't like him down this side of the canal. He's practising with some team-mates."

Cas bounced the ball. "But not you?"

"Uh-uh." Ashley shook his head.

"Your parents don't mind you coming down here?"

"Guess. You've met one of them."

Cas laughed. "That was your dad? I was wondering." He hesitated. "Your mum's black, then?"

"Ten out of ten!"

"Your dad seemed a bit tense."

"He's always like that."

"The sort that'd go ballistic if you crossed him. I shouldn't think he'd be too happy if he discovered you've been coming down here behind his back?"

Ashley slashed his throat with an index finger.

Cas frowned. "He's not Kirkham's headmaster, is he?"

"No, that's Doctor Whitcombe. Sometimes Dad acts like he thinks he is though. He teaches geography."

"Must be difficult, being taught by your dad."

Ashley shrugged. "He only teaches Year Ten and above. He's in charge of Year Eight football though." He kicked at a stone. "I dread Wednesdays."

"What about the girl?"

Ashley frowned. "Which one. Big mouth?"

Cas nodded.

"Light-skinned girl with frizzy hair?"

"Yeah." Cas's face lit up. "The nice-looking one. She got into the car with you."

Ashley kissed his teeth. "You need your eyes testing! That's Laurena — my sister. There's nothing nice about her, looks or otherwise. She fancies herself. She's bossy and she picks on me."

Cas chuckled. "She *picks* on you!"

"Yeah. We don't get on. She's a pain."

"Come on," said Cas, laughing. "You and

I had better scoot or we'll miss the game."

The two boys jogged the rest of the way, dribbling and passing the ball, taking it in turns to sprint ahead.

At the factory yard, quite a crowd had gathered; balls were being kicked back and forth. Gunner emerged from the faces. "All right!" he bellowed, "let's get started. Same captains?"

Boys murmured and nodded. The two captains walked to the fence and flicked a coin.

"Tails!" yelled Gunner, triumphantly. "I pick first. Hands, get over here."

The tall blond goalkeeper sauntered across to Gunner's side.

"Lester." Cas's first choice was the goalkeeper he'd played with before. Lester was stockier and didn't have the reach of Hands. He hadn't been brilliant in that first difficult game, but he'd proved fast on his feet and determined.

"Tony." A broad, mean-looking youth punched the air and swaggered over.

"Kobina." Slim and poised, the African boy walked taller even than Hands.

"I'll have Harris."

"Marsh, then."

"Big End."

"Ash."

"Ash?" There were grunts, guffaws and shouts of "Who's *he*?"

Fourth pick! Ashley was as surprised as the others.

Cas grinned. "Come on, mate, get over here!"

Ashley stepped forward sheepishly, ears burning. He crossed to stand beside his captain.

The names rolled on; the murmurs and

stares faded. Ashley grew restless. Now there would be expectations. He was eager for the game to begin.

It was time for kick-off.

From the start, the pace was relentless. There hadn't been a chance for either side to allocate positions beyond Defence or Attack. As a result, there was always at least half each team running after the ball. With so many players, finding space to manoeuvre was practically impossible. When half-time was called, more than an hour into the game, Cas's team were 7–3 down.

Exhausted and sweating like a pig, Ashley felt miserable. The day was warmer than when he'd played here before. There were more players this time and all of them had been as fresh and rested at the start of the game as him. He had wanted to prove himself, but of their three measly goals, Cas had scored two and Kobina had got the third. Ashley had barely managed the occasional touch.

"You look ready to melt." Cas offered his coke. "There's no modesty here, you know." He gestured.

All around, boys were dragging off their shirts. Ashley stared enviously. There were a variety of shapes and heights, but not a thick waist among them.

He swigged Cas's coke. "Thanks," he said, "I'm fine."

"We've been playing like headless chickens."

Ashley nodded.

"You've got skills." Cas pulled his own shirt up over his head. "You're smart. Slow down and play the clever game. Half these players are bigger than you, and the other half are probably faster!"

"Yeah," Ashley sighed, "you're right!"

Cas smiled. "Work with me, OK?" Clucking and flapping his arms, he strutted off to have words with the others.

Ashley stared. The skin on the back of Cas's arm was crinkled and scarred from wrist to elbow. He shuddered. Something terrible must have happened, yet Cas made no attempt to hide it. He wasn't ashamed or embarrassed.

Hands on hips, Ashley prodded his waist through his shirt. It hadn't shrunk or miraculously vanished, but it hadn't got any thicker. This was ridiculous! Cas wasn't frightened to show his dreadful scars. Why should *he* be embarrassed?

It was time for the sides to change ends and for the second half to get under way. Glancing around to make sure no one was looking, Ashley pulled off his shirt and jogged over to the fence to drape it with the others.

"Ash!"

He turned self-consciously. To his surprise, the ball was already in play and flying towards him. Suddenly, he was running, ball at his feet, hurtling up the right wing. There were only a handful of Gunner's team hanging back and he had passed them already. Cutting in, he aimed for the goal and blasted.

"*Yes!*"

"Thirty seconds into the second half, he scores his first!" Cas came rushing up to him. "That's it. That's what I'm talking about. You found yourself some space."

Others ran over.

"Played!"

"Beautiful pass, Cas."

"But *what a shot!*"

"Nice one, Ash!"

"That's my man!" Cas was jumping up and down. "You see! Some of you doubted me, but I knew after that first game. The boy has class."

Chapter Eight
Argument

THOMAS NODDED. "CATCH you later, Ash."

"Wait! I'll walk with you."

"You're not getting a lift with your dad?"

Ashley glanced heavenward. "Not today, thank God! He's got a meeting to go to."

The two boys walked briskly till they were out of sight of school, then slowed to a dawdle.

"Two goals last week and three this." Ashley had to tell someone.

"Oooh!" Thomas mocked. "Not just a regular in the forbidden zone, but now a star to boot! Do they still keep the same captains?"

Ashley nodded. "Gunner and Cas. Gunner always wins the toss. He and Cas tend to pick the same players from week to week. It's almost as if there were permanent teams."

"Then why bother choosing?"

"It is a bit odd. But not all the regulars have loyalties to one side or the other, a few are happy to float. And players come and go. The set-up seems to suit everyone."

"Gunner's hardly likely to complain,"

Thomas smirked. "Your mob haven't won since you started!"

"Yeah, very funny." Ashley made as if to punch. Thomas ducked. "You should come along, you couldn't do worse than our current goalie."

Thomas shook his head. "I'm not one of your floaters. I tasted victory with Gunner, remember!"

Ashley snorted.

"Why don't *you* volunteer?" said Thomas.

"Don't be a div! For the first time since I can't remember I'm getting the opportunity to play up-front. If they thought I could play in goal, all that would be spoilt. But I'm serious — it'd be a great chance for you."

Thomas looked sheepish. "I'm kind of committed to Trease's weekly practice sessions."

"I'm not sure it's paying off."

"Yeah, sorry about the cock-ups, I don't know what I'm doing at left-back. It makes no sense. But at least I get to do a bit of goalkeeping, when Trease isn't drilling me about this or that defensive strategy. Hey." Thomas halted. "Isn't that Laurena?"

Ashley squinted into the low sun. A group of figures, boys and girls, dithered, laughing and joking, at the crossroads up ahead. He took a few steps. "Yeah, that's her." She was with her usual posse of friends – he recognized faces.

"Isn't that –" Thomas came up beside him – "it is. It's Cas."

Having said their goodbyes, some of Laurena's friends headed away towards Main Street and the bus stops. The remaining group – three girls, Cas, Kobina and Marsh — crossed the road and set off at a brisker pace, down the hill.

"*Come on*," hissed Ashley.

"Are you going to spy on them?" Thomas scurried beside him, close to the wall.

"Spy?" Ashley chuckled. "No, we're just taking the scenic route home."

They followed at a distance. At the bottom of the hill there was a second junction. Beyond, the road turned sharply to run along parallel to the canal. Laurena, Cas and the rest of them walked round the corner and out of sight. Ashley put on a spurt, but by the time he'd rounded the bend, they'd vanished.

Thomas hung back by the turn-off. "This is it for me. I should be home."

"I'm only going as far as the bridge." It

was possible, of course, that Laurena and the others had also taken the turn-off back towards home. But Ashley had a hunch; they'd be somewhere near the water.

"Sorry." Thomas was already shuffling away. "I have to get back."

Ashley would have liked an ally, but there wasn't time to argue. "See you tomorrow, then." He hurried off along the fence that separated the road from the towpath.

The sky was in flames; a fat ruby sun was melting behind the warehouses. This side of the canal, the fence was high and hadn't been vandalized, but there were places where people had pushed their way under. Laurena and the others were nowhere to be seen, so, scrambling under the fence, Ashley dropped down to the towpath.

A chill silence. The canal's dark waters flickered, streaked with blood and fire from the sky. Light was fading, shadows lengthening. Sinister silhouettes of stark buildings loomed in the dusk. Ashley shuddered. He was alone. It was no time to hang about.

He jogged. All the way to the bridge. But saw nobody. Heard nothing. *Where were they?* His mission had failed. He had lost his quarry. It was growing dark. It was time to go home.

Stooping by the steps to pick up some stones, he froze . . . a sudden shriek of laughter. Laurena's voice. No mistaking. From just across the water.

He peered into the gloom. Nothing. Not a sign of anybody. They had to be sitting on the steps, the other side of the bridge. Perhaps they hadn't seen him either? Crouching, cat-like, he crept his way across the bridge.

"Football's boring."

"That's like saying girls are stupid."

"No it's not."

"Yes it is."

"No it's not."

"Perhaps they are then."

"What?"

"Never mind!"

Face to face beneath a street light, Laurena and Cas's eyes blazed. But they were smiling. Gathered around them at the bottom of the steps, the others were laughing and smirking.

"Yo! Cas."

Heads turned.

Ashley peered through the slats of the bridge. He recognized the shout – Gunner, somewhere out there in the gloom.

"We need to have a word, Cas."

"What about?"

"I think you know."

Cas whispered a few words to his mates, then headed off along the towpath. The others followed him with their eyes.

There were two more street lights along the towpath then nothing. As Ashley watched, Cas appeared in the first pool of amber light. Three figures stepped out of the darkness to face him – Gunner, Hands and Big End.

Gunner and Cas began to talk. Their gestures and movements were clear. Ashley could see their mouths moving, he could even hear the sounds of their voices . . . but they were too far off to make out the words. At the end of the bridge the others watched and listened too.

Suddenly, the gestures of the two boys

changed, their voices grew angrier. Gunner was shouting. Cas was shouting back. Hands and Big End stood close behind Gunner.

"Don't just stand there! Get off me!" At the end of the bridge, Laurena struggled to get past Kobina and Marsh. They were both trying to keep her back.

Along the towpath, Gunner pushed Cas. Cas pushed back. Gunner shoved again. Ashley caught his breath. Cas was down and Gunner was standing over him jabbing his finger and bellowing. Ashley jumped up. He wanted to shout, he wanted to race across the bridge and down the towpath . . .

"Stop it!" Breaking free of Kobina and Marsh, Laurena dashed into the darkness along the towpath. Hands and Big End were holding Gunner back. Cas had scrambled back to his feet. He was shouting and waving his fist. He lunged at Gunner, shoved him. Gunner fell.

"Stop it!" Laurena charged between the two youths, pushing Cas back. Gunner leapt to his feet. Kobina and Marsh appeared at Cas's side, fists raised. Three against three. A stand-off! Ashley bit his lip.

Laurena was raging now. "Stupid little boys!" Ashley heard her scream. She shoved Gunner again, then Cas, then each of the youths in turn – Hands, Big End, Kobina, Marsh, then Gunner and Cas once again. Their lowered heads and dropped shoulders said it all.

For several minutes the two groups stood facing each other. Laurena standing in the middle. By their gestures and the tone of their voices, they were in bitter disagreement about something. Laurena was holding sway. Try as he might, Ashley could only recognize the occasional word.

Now Cas and Gunner were both nodding their heads. Laughing and shaking their fists, Gunner and his mates turned and headed off the way they had come. Cas, Laurena, Kobina and Marsh walked back towards the bridge.

"I've had enough!" Laurena snapped, reaching her girlfriends at the bottom of the steps. "We're going home."

Creeping his way back along the bridge, Ashley hurried off into the darkness.

Chapter Nine
Sunday

LAURENA HELD ASHLEY'S gaze across the
dinner table. She had been looking smug
for days. Every time he saw her, he felt the
strongest urge to just come out and *demand*
– who did she think she was, hanging
around with *his* friends? But he couldn't.
He was furious. How dare she?

"I'm going for a wander."

"Oh no you're not, young man."

Ashley stared at his father.

"We've got a crucial match coming up."

Ashley's stomach tightened. "But —"

"Trease has shown great initiative — he'll go far, that boy. He tells me these past few weeks he's taken it upon himself to organize a regular practice in the park. This afternoon you'll be joining them."

"But, Dad . . ."

"No buts." Dad put up his hand. "The big clash against our arch-rivals, Mawdsley, is looming. School pride's at stake! Everyone has to be in tip-top condition. I'll be accompanying you."

Laurena smirked. "Come on, Ash. Dad's right. Anyway," she winked, "it's not as if you do anything with your Sunday afternoons."

She knew!

Laurena swiftly pushed back her chair before he could kick her. "It's a nice day for football in the park." She smiled. "I think I might come along and watch."

It had been a wasted afternoon. Dad doting on Trease and praising his every move and poor old Thomas making a mess of every tackle.

"That's it, Hughes. Go round him, man, go *round* him."

Ashley had made a few good saves, but so what? His heart wasn't in it. Especially with Laurena standing behind him gloating and winding him up whenever Dad was out of ear-shot.

"I think I might go for a stroll in a minute," she had said, "down by the canal . . . I might even cross over the bridge . . . I wonder what I might find? I wonder who I might meet?"

She knew. Ashley checked his watch. Laurena had been gone more than an hour. The factory game would be almost over.

"Keep your eye on the ball," yelled his dad. "No, no, *no,* Moffat. Don't commit till you're *certain*!"

He watched Trease thunder towards him. The bold captain had put a few shots past him this afternoon. But *he* didn't care. Didn't care? He was beyond caring. Trease grinned confidently; arrogantly.

"Don't just stand there with your mouth open!" Dad shook his fist. "What are you going to do, boy? Think! *Do* something!"

He charged . . . low . . . arms outstretched . . . and *dived* . . .

"*Aaaarch!* Aaah . . . ooh . . . aah . . ." Trease writhed and clutched his calf.

"You dirty little —"

"Now, now!" Dad hurried over. "None of that!"

Ashley held out a hand to help Trease up. "What are you on about?"

"Clumsy idiot. *Aah!*" Trease winced and scowled. "You were out of your area."

Ashley glanced around. "I don't see any white lines."

"We're all getting a bit tired." Dad snatched up the ball. "That's probably enough for one day. Next Sunday I think we might give practice a miss. No point risking injuries before the big match."

The factory yard was empty and silent. Why had he bothered to come? He knew they would all have left by now — Cas, Kobina, Gunner, Hands and the rest.

85

Ashley kicked a small piece of glass, turned and headed back towards the bridge. Some Sunday!

Suddenly he heard voices. He listened. No mistaking that laugh. Laurena! *Where was it coming from?* Careful not to make a sound, he took a few steps forward. There it was again! Over to the right – coming from inside the derelict warehouse. He crept towards what had once been a window. A sheet of battered corrugated metal had been pulled back. A hole gaped.

Gripping the ledge and standing on tiptoe, Ashley pulled himself up. He blinked. The air felt cold and damp. It was dark inside. There were noises, not exactly voices – movement . . . breathing. He squinted and tried to focus his eyes. There *was* something. He blinked again.

A shape. A figure. Standing. Long hair

. . . *two heads* . . . one of them looking at him. *Laurena.* Laurena kissing Cas!

He gasped.

"Ashley?"

He dropped.

Inside the warehouse there was a frantic scramble. "Ashley!"

"Get stuffed!" He started to run along the towpath.

"Ashley!"

He looked back over his shoulder. Laurena was out on to the ledge.

"Ash! Come back!"

The pounding of his heart filled his whole chest, a demon fist trying to punch its way out. His lungs burned. He breathed through his lips. Was she out there? Could she hear him? *What was that?*

"Ashley?"

Footsteps.

"Ashley. I know you're in here. I know. Out there is where you've been playing football, isn't it?"

She couldn't tell on him for that. Ashley held his breath. His sister had stuff to hide now. "What d'you want?"

"Just to talk . . . sister to brother . . . as friends . . ."

"That'll be difficult."

"Don't be like that." She was close. "Please?"

He stepped out from behind the wall. "What then?"

Laurena was standing in the shadows. "I want to talk about Cas."

"*My* friend."

"Friends aren't something you *own*."

He clenched his fists. He wanted to hurt her. His heart was still racing. "He's scarred."

"Scarred?"

"Badly. On his arm."

Silence.

He could see her eyes. A questioning look. He nodded. "Did you think that would bother me?" She stepped into the light. "Little brother, I already knew." She came forward. "He got burned. There was a fire at Sedgefield Comp. Cas, along with three others, was accused of starting it."

"Arson!" Ashley stared, stunned. Arson was serious. People got sent to prison. "How do you know?"

"Cas told me." Laurena sighed. "He says he didn't do it. He was with the others, but he tried to stop them. He got burned trying to put it out when the others had all run off."

"He could be lying."

Laurena shrugged. "Obviously someone thought so."

"How d'you mean?"

"He was found guilty."

Ashley's mouth felt dry.

"Cas was expelled," said Laurena. "He was given community service and a suspended sentence like the others. He's furious – he's missed months of school. He'll have to start the whole year again somewhere new. He's applied to Kirkham."

Ashley checked his sister's face. This wasn't a wind-up.

"They had an argument," she continued, "Cas and the other three – Hands and another white boy called Big End, I think, and Gunner. He's the main one, a nasty piece of work. D'you know them?"

Ashley nodded.

"It turned into a bit of a fight. I had to break it up. They were really going for each other. Cas was furious. He challenged Gunner."

"*Challenged* him?"

"Next Sunday there's going to be a special match – here in the factory yard. There's three hundred pounds at stake."

"Three hundred pounds!" Ashley couldn't believe his ears.

"Apparently. Cas doesn't have any money, but that's what he'll have to find. If he loses he has to pay them a hundred pounds each."

"He must be crazy."

"Maybe." Laurena raised an eyebrow. "But if Cas wins, Gunner and his mates have agreed to write a confession telling the truth – how he was the one who tried to put out the Sedgefield fire. And how he had nothing to do with starting it."

"Will they do that?"

"Why shouldn't they? They've already been found guilty so it's no skin off their noses." Laurena sighed. "But for Cas, it's everything. He *has* to win."

Footsteps.

Laurena turned.

"Hello?" Cas appeared. "Here you are. I was looking."

Ashley nodded.

Cas smiled. "All right mate?"

Ashley nodded again.

"Am I interrupting?"

"We were just having a little chat," said Laurena.

Ashley smiled. "Brother and sister stuff."

"I see." Cas patted the football he was clutching. "We missed you today."

"Sorry, I had to do stuff."

Cas shrugged. "We lost, of course."

Ashley smiled. "Of course!"

"But what about next Sunday? There's a bit of a special match on. It's really important. I need you – can you play?"

"Ash, what about Dad?" Laurena glanced at Cas. "Dad might make him join the practice in the park again."

"That's not going to happen," said Ashley.

"Oh no?" Laurena smirked.

Cas ignored her. "You sure, Ash?"

"Positive."

"I can count on you?"

Ashley nodded.

"Great!" Cas grinned. "I've a little favour to ask."

"What?" Ashley grinned back.

"I need you in goal."

Chapter Ten
Factory-yard Match

"IF YOU'RE NEEDED," Cas had said, "play rush." Fat chance!

"*Gwaaan!*"

The onslaught had been relentless, practically non-stop. And, for much of that time, the area around their goal had been the front line. Ashley was in the thick of it. The war zone.

"Block him! Tackle!"

All this time and no score, *all this time at such a pace*. It was incredible. Both sides were growing desperate. Carelessness and clumsiness were creeping into the game.

But the ball kept coming. There was never time to stop and take stock. Voices all round – yelling, shouting, barking. Aggressive voices, panicky voices, *loud* voices.

Here came the ball again.

"*Gwaaan!*" Laurena screeched, over by the fence. "Psyche him, Ash!"

"*Yes!*" Thomas cheered. "Brilliant! Saved!"

"And again, Ash." Cas was back with him, trying to get the ball away. "Come on, you can do it. *Yes!*"

"Back on your feet, mate."

"*Saved!*"

"Nice one!"

Fight the distractions. Eye on the ball.

"Uh-oh, here it comes again. Quick, get ready Ashley!"

"You can do it, mate. Come on."

At last!

At last, the ball was safe in his hands. He was in control. Ashley gulped. He wanted to slow his lungs, but they kept heaving. His *heart*! He wanted to slow down time, stretch out the few precious seconds he could hold the ball. He wanted to *recover*. He couldn't remember ever feeling like this – this frantic, this exhausted.

Boys pushed, barged and jostled each other. Directly in front of him, Smidge, their tiny midfielder, flitted between the others, looking for space. Ashley ducked and swerved – grim Harris and ugly Big

End were in his face, trying to obstruct and intimidate. He twisted, rolling the ball out to skinny Marsh. It bounced and skipped, but, by a miracle, got there. Marsh took off. Up the wing. With a prayer.

"Go, Marshie, *go*!"

Gunner led the pack, on his tail.

Cas ran straight up the middle.

Marsh drew them. Doubled back, sharply. Hooked it round and over their heads, looping into the centre . . .

. . . a great ball . . .

Cas tapped it on, left to Kobina. Defenders raced over to cover. Running with it ten paces, Kobina pushed it across . . . Cas accelerated . . . *bang!*

"*YES!*"

The old one-two.

"Goal!"

At last.

"One–nil!"

"Played!" Jogging back, Marsh saluted him. "That was totally mental – but it worked!"

"Now's the critical moment." Ashley slapped his palms together. "They'll be coming twice as hard."

"Here we go," Marsh grunted. "They don't intend to let us have a breather."

Smidge and Kobina were still celebrating, deep in enemy territory.

"Get back!" yelled Ashley.

"It's not a holiday!" roared Cas. "They're not going to wait for us. Come on – move! Don't slacken now."

But Gunner and his mob were already forward. Placing the ball on the centre spot, Big End tapped it into play.

"*Get back*!" Ashley whistled his defenders. "Mark up!"

Arms pumping like pistons, Gunner led the charge. One goal down, his troops were hungry for revenge. Big End to his right, long-haired wild man Harris, on the outside. A three-pronged attack breaking through the midfield. They fanned out, pursued by a rabble. Where would they strike?

Force a move. Bravery time. Out to meet them.

Exploding off the line, Ashley charged. "*Grrrrraaaaaaaaaah!* Come on, then! *Come on!*"

For a brief, shocked moment, Gunner appeared to lose his stride. He staggered, arms windmilling, then flicked the ball wide. "Yours!"

Harris bore down hard.

Ashley swerved. He was too far out now to turn back. It was him or Harris.

"*Gwaaan!*"

Neck and neck.

Impact!

He lurched left, jumping Harris's hip . . . landed running and . . . *took flight*. Gunner to the left of him, the rest to his right.

"Excellent, Ash!" Cas was boxed in. "Get rid of it now and get back!"

Ashley glanced around for someone to give it to — he had come out almost to the centre! A little chip over heads and through to collect. Then, one touch lofted the ball neatly to Kobina behind enemy lines. Perfect.

"Don't just stand there!" Gunner was furious with his wrong-footed backs. "*Bring him down!*"

Kobina hurtled towards the goal, half a dozen players on his tail.

Hurrying back to his own goal, Ashley watched evil-eyed Curtis home in.

"Kobina," yelled Cas, "to your left — *man on!*"

Kobina blasted and — "Aaa-aaaagh!" — shrieked, as flying Curtis chopped away his leg. The keeper punched the shot clear.

Marshie caught the ball in his hands.

Suddenly, everyone was shouting at once. The whole pitch rushed towards the same spot.

"Foul!"

"Get lost!"

"It was deliberate! Anyone could see."

"Don't be stupid!"

"You're scum, Curtis!"

"You want to make something of it?"

Ashley raced up the pitch. The situation looked ugly. Players were pushing each other and waving their arms. Cas was bending over his groaning, injured player. Marshie, still with the ball in his hands was backing away from Gunner, Hands and others. Shaking their fists, they were demanding the ball. Everyone was yelling.

"LEAVE IT!" Cas's furious roar froze everybody. He lifted Kobina's bloodied leg, and turned his blazing eyes on Curtis.

Curtis smirked. "I was going for the ball. I *swear*."

"Sure." Cas spat at the ground. He looked over at Gunner. "Well?"

Gunner was smirking too. "Accidents happen. If you play with the big boys, sometimes you get hurt."

"You're pathetic!" Cas snarled. "Kobina's lucky nothing's broken. Bringing him down like that, *on concrete*, was totally out of order. That's a penalty."

Gunner glared. "Over my dead body."

"Don't tempt me." Cas pushed past him to Marsh.

Cas turned with the ball in his hands. The two boys were face to face. The others gathered. Was there going to be a fight?

Ashley glanced round at Laurena. Behind the fence with the other spectators, this time she was powerless to intervene.

Cas thrust his face close to Gunner's. "It's a *penalty*."

Gunner snarled. "We don't have them!"

"This is different."

"No exceptions." They were staring furiously, nose to nose. "Play on, or *quit*."

"Quit?" Cas glanced at his watch. "No way!" He snorted. "You're finished! You'll never equalize now!"

"Let's see!" Snatching the ball from Cas's arms, Gunner hurled it into the air. "Play on!"

Everybody scrambled – some after the ball, some for position. Chaos. A mad scrum.

The ball went straight to Big End.

"Get back, Ashley, run!"

Ashley jerked around – he was well into the opposition half! Gunner's team were running with the ball. He *sprinted*.

"Go, Ashley, *faster*."

He glanced behind. Harris had the ball. Cas was right on his heels. Everyone was charging up the yard. *Come on*. He drove his legs faster.

"Shoot!"

From the corner of his eye, Ashley saw Harris swerve and kick. The ball was in the air. A steep lob.

Faster, he begged his legs. *Please! Faster!*
The ball sailed above him. He charged.
Arms outstretched, he dived . . .

Chapter Eleven
Honour

LAURENA POPPED HER head round the door.

Ashley scowled. "What d'you want?"

"I just came to wish you luck." She stepped into the room. "How are the wounds?"

He touched his chin. "*Ow!* I think the

nurses left some grit in."

"We'll have to call you Rock-jaw."

"No thanks."

"How about the knees?"

"I can jog – just about."

"How about crouching?"

He shook his head. "Agony."

Laurena smiled. "I'm sure you'll do fine."

"What are *you* after?"

She frowned. "How d'you mean?"

"You're being nice."

She sat on the bed. "Ashley, I know you and I don't always get on."

"Huh!"

"Sometimes I can be a bit of a cow."

"You said it."

"Thank you!" She pulled a sarcastic face. "You're not so perfect, you know."

He glowered. "Huh!"

"But you've improved." She smiled. "You stood up to Dad."

He looked away.

"I don't know if you've changed, or if I'm just seeing you differently, but I used to think you were so . . . spineless."

"Oh — *thanks!*"

"But I don't any more. That's what I wanted to tell you. After the business with Dad, and then watching you play last Sunday, I've decided you must be pretty brave."

Ashley stared. If he had changed, he wasn't the only one — this wasn't the Laurena he was used to. "This isn't a trick?"

"Cross my heart."

He sighed and fiddled with his finger ends. "Will you tell me something?"

"Ask away."

"The last few Sundays down at the factory yard, Cas has picked me as a forward."

"I know, he told me."

"Was he just flattering me as a way of getting in with you?"

"No." She touched his leg. "He was *dead impressed* with your skills. I was shocked when he said so. I thought he was winding me up, till I watched you on Sunday." She smiled. "You're right to stand up to Dad, he shouldn't make you play keeper if you don't want to. You looked easily good enough out of goal. Believe me, Cas wasn't *using* you."

"Thanks."

Blowing his whistle, the referee pointed sharply to the spot.

"Oh, come on, ref!" From the touchline,

Dad put on his usual display. Dr Whitcombe and Mr Phillips, the Head of Sport, nodded approvingly. This was a very important match. County talent spotters were rumoured to be present.

The ref was right, of course, Thomas had been way too slow on the tackle. But this was all they needed – a disaster, only minutes from half-time.

Unsurprisingly, the striker who had scored Mawdsley's goal, lined up to take the penalty. Ashley tried to read his face.

"Don't let me down this time, Ashley." Dad's voice quivered with threat. "Come on, Kirkham!"

"Put it away, Sanjay!"

The pitch went quiet.

The boy ran so lightly he seemed to float.

Ashley sprang. His knees screamed. The

ball shot past his finger tips . . . into the back of the net.

"*GOAL!*"

He struggled to his feet. Blood was seeping from the plasters on his knees, soaking into his socks.

"Come on, Kirkham," Dad glared furiously. "One before the whistle, that's all I ask. We're not beaten yet!"

Trease took the kick. But his long ball was too ambitious. Mawdsley's flame-haired sweeper intercepted, and a line of blue shirts began to advance.

"*Idiot*, Trease!" Dad had blown a fuse. Red-faced and flapping, he hopped up and down. "Get back! Get that ball back!"

Mawdsley's forwards passed tightly, pushing their way through the midfield.

"Don't stand there!" Dad roared. "Don't

wait for them to stomp all over you. *Do* something!"

Behind Ganesh, the midfielder, Moffat and Barnett crept forward uncertainly.

"Get stuck in, Barny!" Ashley tested his knees with a gentle crouch. "Take him on, Thomas . . ."

Ganesh hurried, arms flailing. The ball was tapped sideways, their striker ran on to it.

Barnett made his move too late. The advancing blue line didn't even have to slow. The striker accelerated.

Thomas, watching for his moment, went in, *hard*.

"Played!"

A good clean tackle.

Both players were down. The ball was rolling loose across the penalty area.

Ashley charged. Three Mawdsley

forwards were closer than him, but to get to the ball, each had to slow and change direction. He could beat them. He was travelling in a straight line – "Go Ashley, GO!" – like a bullet.

"Go on, Ash! You can do it!" It was Laurena! Howling from the other side of the pitch.

"*Yes!*"

Got it. By a cat's whisker. Ball at his feet, he was still accelerating. Blues to the right and left, open space ahead – the only sensible thing to do was *keep going*. His legs felt like liquid. They were moving so fast they scarcely felt part of him. He glanced around for someone to pass to.

In front of him, Trease struggled to shake off his shadow. "Pass it out!" he yelled pointing to the wing.

Ashley ran on. All he could see was blue shirts. Across on the other wing, Rawlinson was boxed in by his marker. There was nothing else for it. Swerving to avoid a tackle, he cut right and crossed the centre line.

"What d'you think you're *doing*?" Dad's loud voice boomed across the pitch. "You're in Mawdsley's half. Are you out of your mind? Get rid of it, boy! Get back in your area!"

Easy to say! Two blue shirts hovered for the kill. Ashley dodged left then right, crashing into the second and knocking him over. He thundered on. Rawlinson sprinting in front from the wing, Trease on his inside, but blocked by two. Ashley lofted the ball up and over.

Blues on his tail, Rawlinson caught the

ball with his head, brought it down and –
"Yours!" – passed it straight back.

Whack! From the edge of the box,
Ashley booted it, first touch.

"*GOAL!*"

"Unbelievable!"

"Magnificent!"

The whistle had blown for the goal and
half-time. Ashley's head was buzzing.

"Wicked shot!"

"Way to go!"

"Nice one!"

One by one, Hughes, Rawlinson,
Thomas, Barny and the rest of his team-
mates hugged or patted him on the
back.

Trease gave a nod. "I never knew you
had it in you."

Dad glowered as they walked to the
touchline.

"Very unconventional," Dr Whitcombe beamed, "but a goal nevertheless!"

Mr Phillips held out his hand. "Terrific run, terrific shot, son."

Dad stared, speechless.

"We've got to get your boy out there, scoring for us, John." Dr Whitcombe beckoned.

Ashley approached, avoiding Dad's eyes.

"We can't leave such talent locked up in goal." Dr Whitcombe was adamant. "Who's your reserve, Ashley?"

"Moffat, sir." Ashley pointed to Thomas.

"Any good?"

"Yes, sir." Ashley glanced at his plastered knees. "Under the circumstances, probably better than me."

Dr Whitcombe nodded. "Mr Grant, I suggest you make some rapid rearrangements. Put Ashley up-front. We need goals. We must *not* lose. Do I make myself clear?"

Dad's face twitched. He nodded.

Exhausted, Ashley jogged back across the line. Since scoring the equalizer, he had felt like a moving target. Every time he received the ball, blue shirts were on him like flies.

Trease wasn't helping any. Furious at being ousted from the front line, he kept barking contradictory instructions. He was playing with two left feet.

Time was running out. The Mawdsley team pressed forward, passing as tightly as ever.

Find one last burst.

He lurched, charged and — "*Yes!*" — the ball was his.

"Come on, Kirkham!" Dr Whitcombe bellowed. "Come *on!*"

Ashley passed the ball across to Hughes and accelerated through the blues looking for clear space. The ball came back over the blues' heads. Beautiful pass! Perfect. He ran on.

Suddenly, it felt like he couldn't put a foot wrong. It was amazing – the opposition seemed to slow, their tackles became hesitant. They were afraid!

Hughes had found himself a channel and was powering through on the inside. Rawlinson had come round wide. Ashley tapped the ball left, and swerved right. Hughes knocked it on to the wing. They were steaming! Nothing could stop them now!

"Get back!" The blues were panicking. "Come on, Mawdsley, find your concentration!"

Ashley was in their area. He glanced

ahead — Mawdsley's goalie crouched, watching Rawlinson out on the wing. He'd been there, he knew that feeling.

The pass came high. Three blue shirts jumped, one after another. Hughes leaped too . . .

But this ball had *his* name on it. Ashley dived.

"*Goal!*"

The whistle blew. And again. Long shrill blasts.

Victory.

"Congratulations!" Dr Whitcombe beamed and held out his hand. "These two gentlemen talent-spot for the county."

"Spectacular header, son."

"Thank you." Ashley shook their hands.

"Marvellous game. Congratulations."

Mr Phillips patted him on the head. "I

think Mister Grant's been hiding his son's talent under a bushel."

The talent scouts looked baffled.

"Young Ashley here is the team coach's son," explained Dr Whitcombe. "Mister Grant probably kept Ashley from the striker's job because he was trying to avoid favouritism." He slapped Dad on the back. "That right?"

Dad nodded, sheepishly.

"You should be proud, Mister Grant, your boy's a star."

"Ashley!"

He turned. Laurena was hurrying towards them, a posse of her friends behind. She smiled and waved. Cas was by her side.

"You were brilliant, Ash!" She gave him a big hug. "I knew you could do it!" she whispered.

Cas slapped his palm. "Result!"

"Sorry for butting in, sir." Laurena nodded apologetically to Dr Whitcombe.

"No, well deserved." Dr Whitcombe gestured. "Please, carry on."

"Dad." Laurena tugged Cas forward. "Dad, this is Cas."

Dad stiffened and scowled.

Laurena smiled. "Cas has been helping Ashley develop his skills as a striker." She twisted round and held out her hand. Ashley took it. "Encouraging him to come forward."

"Excellent chap!" Dr Whitcombe patted Cas on the back. "A bit of initiative." He turned to the others. "Just yesterday we accepted young Cas here as a pupil at Kirkham. Comes with a splendid school record in class and on the field. He'll be starting on Monday."

Ashley grinned. He felt giddy.

"Now then." Dr Whitcombe draped an arm around Dad's shoulders. "You've been a little tight-lipped through all this. I think a little congratulation is in order, don't you?"

Dad cleared his throat. "Thank you," he croaked, nodding to Laurena and Cas.

Ashley met his glance.

"Well done, son."